Dolphin Freedom

Dolphin Freedom

Wayne Grover

Illustrated by Jim Fowler

HarperTrophy®
A Division of HarperCollinsPublishers

Dolphin Freedom
Text copyright © 1999 by Wayne Grover
Illustrations copyright © 1999 by Jim Fowler

Library of Congress Cataloging-in-Publication Data
Grover, Wayne.
 Dolphin freedom / by Wayne Grover; pictures by Jim Fowler.
 p. cm.
 Summary: A diver and his friends rescue a family of dolphins from Bahamian poachers
who are selling the dolphins to marine parks.
 ISBN 0-380-73305-6 (pbk.)
 1. Dolphins—Juvenile fiction. [1. Dolphins—Fiction. 2. Poaching—Fiction.
3. Wildlife rescue—Fiction. 4. Bahamas—Fiction.]
I. Fowler, Jim ill. II. Title.
PZ10.3.G8875Do 1999   98-5384
[Fic]—dc21   CIP
                                                                  AC

First Harper Trophy edition, 2000
❖
Visit us on the World Wide Web!
www.harperchildrens.com

*For the thousands of children across America
who share their love of dolphins with me.
It is your happy faces and bright minds
that let me know my writing matters.*
—W. G.

For Jimmy, Ricky, Daryn, and Quentin
—J. F.

Contents

Chapter One

The Dolphin Poachers

The little white dog paddled furiously as she tried to keep up with the large dolphin. *Woof! Woof!* She let him know she wanted some attention. The dolphin rolled over on his side and repeatedly slapped the water with his right pectoral fin, his bottlenose seeming to smile at the game.

As the little dog began to tire and sink lower, the dolphin disappeared and, with a rush of clear

Atlantic water, came up under her, picking her up on his back. As he did, another little white dog jumped from the boat bow and landed with a splash. She did her best dog paddle and soon joined them, barking as she swam.

We were anchored about a mile off the coast of Palm Beach, Florida, and for about fifteen minutes the dolphin took turns carrying the dogs around in the water. Baby loved to play and take them for rides on his broad gray back, even though they were never quite sure if they liked to go so fast. Baby sensed their discomfort and chirped in delight as he swam in a big circle, always bringing them back to me as I sat on the swim platform with my feet in the water.

It was always a wonderful experience, and I never worried about sharks bothering the dogs, because Baby's dolphin family provided a ring of safety nothing could get through.

"Okay, Baby, we've got to go home now," I called to the large male Atlantic bottlenose dolphin who has been my companion on nearly every dive and outing I've been on since I rescued him as a two-month-old baby years ago.

I wanted to get my boat, the *Treasure Hunter*, back to the dock to pick up a new piece of high-tech navigational equipment called a Global Positioning Satellite (GPS), which uses satellites overhead to determine a boat's location within ten feet of its actual position on the water.

"Bambi, Blossom, come here," I called to my two dogs. They turned and swam to the platform on the back of the boat, and I lifted them on board.

As I started the engines, Mama, Papa, Bluebell, Scarback, and Angel, members of Baby's family, joined us alongside the boat and stayed with us until we pulled into the Intracoastal Waterway. There they stopped. The dolphins usually don't like getting too close to boats and other signs of civilization—something I was thankful for because they could get hurt in the heavy boat traffic.

At the dock, a Florida Marine Patrol officer walked over and gave me some disturbing news. "We've had reports that a Bahamas-based dolphin-poaching operation has been seen netting dolphins off South Florida. They are using Zodiac rubber boats to chase them down. I knew you would like to know, considering your buddies out there."

I thanked him for the warning, then tried to put it out of my mind. But I couldn't help worrying about Baby and his family.

The next afternoon my longtime friend and diving partner, Amos, the dogs, and I went out onto the ocean to correlate the GPS with our various diving location sites for future use. Amos didn't dive much anymore because of his arthritis, but he was still the best seaman I had ever known.

As we turned out of the inlet, I was mildly surprised that no dolphins joined us. They'll come in a few minutes, I thought to myself. It was a beautiful day with calm seas, blue skies, and puffy white clouds. The beauty of it always thrilled me.

"Amos, the dolphins don't seem to be around today," I said, a little concerned.

Amos, his eyes squinting in a face nearly leather after fifty years in the sun, was scanning the water around us. We'd always figured the dolphins recognized the particular sound of our boat's powerful engines and came to us because no two boats sound alike.

Amos and I had named the dolphins one by one as we got to know them, and over time each dolphin learned to respond when called individually. Whenever we pulled one of our two boats out into the open sea from the waterway, the whole dolphin family joined us, sometimes bringing along as many as twenty dolphin friends.

They loved to race along with us and play in the bow waves, especially Baby. Since I had saved his life by cutting a large fishhook from his body, we had developed a unique man-dolphin relationship—a friendship that few people ever experience or understand.

Bambi and Blossom, both bichon frise females with curly white coats, always wore little red life vests my wife had sewn for them. Whenever I went scuba diving, they would both stay on the boat, lying on the bow, watching for me to reappear.

My wife had made them pink bonnets and insisted I tie them on to keep the dogs from getting sunburned eyes and noses. The dogs in their bonnets were a sight that made everyone laugh. Even the dolphins that surfaced and chattered to them from their watery home seemed to be grinning. It was not unusual for Bambi to bark while the dolphins stood high on their tails and bobbed their heads in unison, like church deacons dressed in black suits with white shirts.

Bambi, at fourteen, is top dog and Blossom, at six, is underdog, a ranking each follows carefully.

Bambi likes swimming with the dolphins so much I have to be sure she doesn't overdo it. On this day, I smiled as I thought about all the fun times we had had with Baby, still wondering why he and his dolphin family hadn't joined us yet.

As I tested the GPS, Amos grunted, "Dadburned little black boxes." He hated the idea of the gadget and never let me forget it.

"Relax, Amos, I just want to test this thing using your visual landmarks for correlation. I still trust your eyes, old friend," I assured him.

Amos is my best friend, and I trust him with my life, but technology now gives sailors a better way to stay on course. But I don't want to hurt Amos's pride by saying so.

I turned the boat south and pushed the throttles to about 80 percent full. The *Treasure Hunter*'s bow raised as the engines roared with pure power. We were going so fast the boat was skipping along the small wave tops, throwing onto the deck a cold salty bath that the dogs did their best to avoid.

There were many other boats at sea that day:

fishing boats, yachts coming from and going to exotic places, sailboats leaning over with full sails, and pleasure boats of every shape and size.

Farther out, I saw a sleek yacht with two Zodiac rubber rafts buzzing around it like bees. "Uh-oh," I said. I raised my binoculars to see better.

The boats were nearly a mile away, and I could not see exactly what they were doing, but the fast little rubber Zodiacs, each with two men, were racing along after something.

Then I saw something that made my heart stop. Just ahead of the lead Zodiac, I saw a dolphin arc out of the water, with the sun glistening on its smooth back.

"Amos, those are the poachers!"

He frowned and jerked the wheel to the left as the boat made a sharp turn. "Well, they ain't gonna get any dolphins as long as I'm around," Amos said.

We sped toward the three boats, quickly closing the distance.

As we neared, I saw the Zodiacs close on each

side of a dolphin, with a man in each boat hold-ing an end of a large net. Then the net was thrown over the animal, trapping it. The boats quickly stopped, and the men dragged the netted dolphin alongside. I could see it struggling to free itself, and I could hear it frantically calling out in terror.

"Amos, get closer to those rafts," I shouted above the sound of the engines.

He steered straight for the two rafts, and within seconds we were upon them.

The four men looked surprised. They had been so busy trying to capture the dolphin that they did not see us coming.

I was enraged! It is against the law to capture wild dolphins, but we all knew it was done by shady operators who sold them to marine parks, where the dolphins live in concrete ponds and perform for tourists.

"Let that animal go . . . NOW!" I ordered.

One of the men looked over at me with a scowl on his face. "Get out of here! This is none of your business," he snarled.

"Take that net off the dolphin and let it go!" I repeated.

"Look, buddy, I'm warning you," he threatened. "Just get out of here before you get hurt."

Amos stood by my side and said in a low, angry tone, "You heard the man. Let that dolphin go! I've called the Coast Guard, and they're on the way."

Just then the large mother boat radioed the

Zodiacs. The head man in the main boat knew the situation was out of control and ordered his capture boats to leave the scene.

We all heard the transmission: "Drop the nets and let's get out of here!"

The men in the nearest boat threw the nets overboard, right onto the dolphin, already struggling to stay afloat with the weight of the heavy net pulling it down so its blowhole was underwater.

"Don't!" I shouted, too late.

The scared dolphin was now completely underwater and sinking fast. I knew it could drown in a minute or two. Amos wanted to chase the boats as they raced away toward the mother craft, but he knew we had to act immediately to save the dolphin. Bambi and Blossom sensed the excitement and barked at the action.

I quickly slipped off my deck shoes and jumped into the water toward the place where the dolphin was struggling. I didn't know what I could do, but I was not going to let that dolphin drown without trying to help.

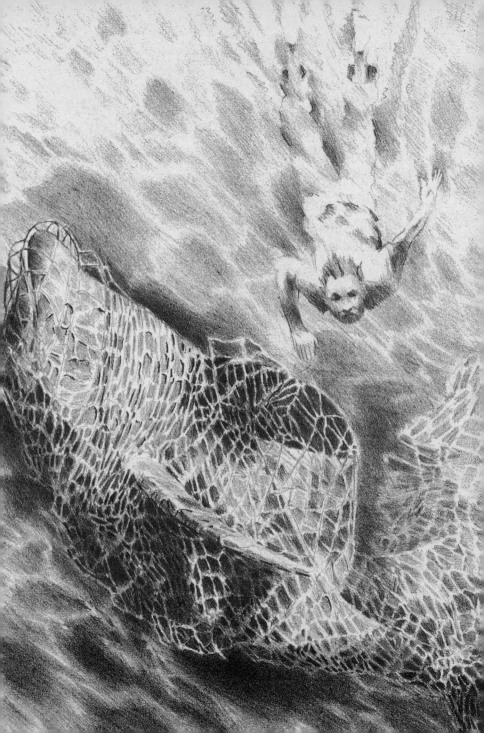

Looking down into the clear water beneath me, I saw the poor dolphin trying to free itself, to no avail. The more it struggled, the more entangled it became.

Taking a deep breath, I dived directly toward it. Without a mask, my eyes burned from the salty water, and all I could see was a blurry outline of a dolphin and tangled nets. I swam deeper and deeper as the dolphin, unable to swim, sank quickly toward the ocean bottom, about a hundred and fifty feet below.

My lungs were bursting. I had not taken enough breath to dive, and I was already short of breath from the anger and confrontation with the poachers.

Down, down I went. At about fifty feet, I reached out and grabbed a handful of net. We continued to sink, and I gave a mighty tug to stop us. I grabbed the net in my teeth to free my arms for swimming and struggled to swim upward with the heavy load. The dolphin stopped struggling and watched me through the net.

My heart pounded, and for a moment, I thought I must either let go or drown too. I tried desperately to reach the surface. I had no idea how far it was back up because I couldn't see clearly.

I heard the boat's engines above, and I knew Amos was close at hand. It seemed like minutes as I swam with all my strength.

Just as I was going to let go of the net, my head burst from the water. I took a deep breath.

Amos had the boat only a few feet away. He knew exactly what to do. He used a rope-grabbing hook and snagged the net, pulling the dolphin and me alongside.

The exhausted dolphin was blowing sharply through its blowhole, and I saw its eyes rolling as it tried to see where it was.

"It's okay, friend, I'll free you," I said softly as I carefully tried to unwrap the nets from the tired mammal.

The more I tried, the worse it got. "Amos, give me a knife," I called.

He leaned over the side and handed me a

large knife. I cut away the tough net as the dolphin trembled in fear.

I kept talking gently as I worked, and within a few moments, the last of the net fell away. With a mighty flip of its tail, the dolphin shot away and dived beneath the sea.

"You're welcome," I called after it.

Amos helped me back into the boat. As I sat down, panting for breath, Amos said, "Pretty close there, Wayne."

"Closer than you think," I replied.

The three boats had almost disappeared to the south as I looked around for them.

"The Zodiacs didn't have any registration numbers, and I couldn't see the main boat's numbers either," Amos said with a sigh. "But I saw the name on the stern. It was the *Big Blue* out of Nassau."

"Those guys really burn me up," I said. "What if they captured Baby or some of his family?"

Almost before the words were out, I felt a deep sense of dread. Baby had not missed meeting us once in six months—and today he had.

"You thinking what I am, Wayne?"

"Yes, I am! You know Baby lets boats come close, and we've taught him to trust people. Do you suppose that boat took some dolphins before we interrupted?"

If my dolphin friend had been captured for some dolphin show, it would be my fault. I picked up Bambi and held her close as we turned and headed into the inlet.

Blossom stood on her back legs, front paws on my knees, wagging her tail back and forth. She wanted equal time on my lap.

"Baby probably was out deep-sea fishing today. We'll see her tomorrow," my old friend said, trying to comfort me, but neither of us believed it.

As I lay down to sleep that night with my wife, Barbara, by my side and the exhausted dogs sleeping at our feet, I kept picturing Baby, trapped and scared, away from his family and distressed that a human had turned his freedom into captivity.

I could just imagine his pain and disbelief that humans had taken him from his home in the open sea. Dolphins live in tight-knit family groups called pods and care for one another for life. If the poachers had Baby, who knew how many more of his family had been captured?

Before I drifted off to sleep, I promised myself I would learn more about the dolphin-hunting operation we had tangled with that day.

Chapter Two

Baby is Captured

The next morning I called the Florida Marine Patrol and explained what Amos and I had seen.

Sergeant Bob Taylor let out a long sigh and said, "We have been trying to catch those guys for a month now. They are out of the Bahamas and have been poaching dolphins for a chain of two-bit marine amusement parks in Mexico.

"I was told they get more than five thousand

dollars per animal delivered alive to a holding area on a small island southwest of Bimini. They were poaching in the Gulf of Mexico last year when we caught them. Of the eight dolphins on board, five were dead and one was so sick it died before we could get help.

"We released the other two into the gulf. Turns out the guys were fined five hundred bucks apiece and let go. Evidently they are working the Atlantic Coast this year. We're really short-handed and can't patrol all the waterways, so they can elude us most of the time."

"What can I do to stop them if I should see them again?" I asked.

"Be very careful. Those guys are dangerous and would shoot you if they thought they could get away with it. Leave the law to us! Okay?"

I hesitated a moment, then said, "Okay." But in my heart I knew I was going to stop those crooks one way or another.

A strong wind was blowing up large waves, preventing Amos and me from going to sea to look for Baby and his family. So I spent the day calling Florida marine parks to see what they knew about dolphin poachers. I knew they obtained their dolphins and whales legally.

They all told me they had been approached by the dolphin snatchers at one time or another and had turned them down. When I called Sea World, near Orlando, one of the managers told me where to look for missing dolphins.

She told me about Dead Man Cay, a small island on the western coast of the Bahamas. I shuddered to think of the once happy and free dolphins trapped in small, dirty tanks, being fed dead fish. I knew where Dead Man Cay was, and I wanted to go there as soon as possible to search for the captured dolphins.

A call to the Coast Guard let me know that Dead Man Cay was a hangout for ex-cons and international crooks who had a very bad reputation for giving strangers a hard time. I knew this was not going to be easy.

The next morning the sea was smooth with just a breath of wind stirring.

Amos had to work his regular job, so I took

the *Treasure Hunter* out by myself. Bambi and Blossom sat next to me as I steered from the flying-bridge wheel, about ten feet above the boat's deck. From that position I could see farther.

I left the inlet with both engines roaring and turned south along the coast. When I approached the area where Baby and his family usually came to meet us, I was relieved to see a school of dolphins headed my way.

Maybe I was concerned for nothing, I chided myself as the dolphins came closer. I pulled the throttles closed, and the boat slowed. I could see five . . . no, six dolphins arcing through the water toward me. Bambi wagged her tail as she watched them come closer.

I climbed down to the main deck and stood looking over the port side. Bambi tried to peer over the side, but she was too small, so I picked her up and held her in my arms as I watched for Baby to appear. Blossom jumped up on the bow and wagged her tail happily.

One by one, I recognized each one of the dolphins like the old friends they were. Each had distinct characteristics, markings, scars, or shapes.

Old Scarback came near the boat and lay quiet in the water just below me. Then Baby's father, the one we called Papa, did the same.

They were strangely quiet. Usually they chirped and played like happy children.

Today they just looked up at me. Papa made a low sound, almost like a moan. He did it again. I had never heard a dolphin make that sound before.

I put Bambi on the deck and reached down to touch Papa and Scarback, but they moved away from my hand. I reached out as far as I could, but they stayed just out of touching range. I knew it immediately. They didn't trust me anymore.

"Papa, Scarback, what's wrong?" I asked quietly.

Papa looked up at me and made the moaning sound again. Scarback joined him. It was a pitiful sound that broke my heart.

I looked at the gathered dolphins for Baby's mother, but she was missing too. So were Baby's sisters, Bluebell and Angel.

"Papa, where is Baby?" I asked.

He lay still and moaned again. As I looked closer, I saw a bloody hole near his right pectoral fin. He was in pain. Someone or something had stuck Papa and hurt him badly.

I was so angry I felt the blood rush to my face. I threw an anchor over the bow and told the dogs, "Stay!"

I stepped onto the swim platform and slid

into the water. The dolphins moved close together as I swam near them, bunching up for safety and to protect Papa.

Dolphins have rarely been known to attack a human, even when they are being threatened. But I knew that these dolphins had been frightened by the poachers, and I had to be careful. They could certainly defend themselves with their sharp teeth or ram into me as they do with sharks that attack a member of their pod.

I talked to the dolphins gently as I tried to get close. Scarback came forward and met me head-on, placing himself between me and the group. I treaded water and talked to him. "I know you have lost some of your family, and I see that Papa is hurt. I am your friend; you know that. Let me examine Papa's wounds."

Scarback did not budge. I tried to swim around him, but he moved too, staying between me and his family.

I remembered when I had first met the dolphin family on a dive, when Baby's mother and father had brought him to me as a small baby,

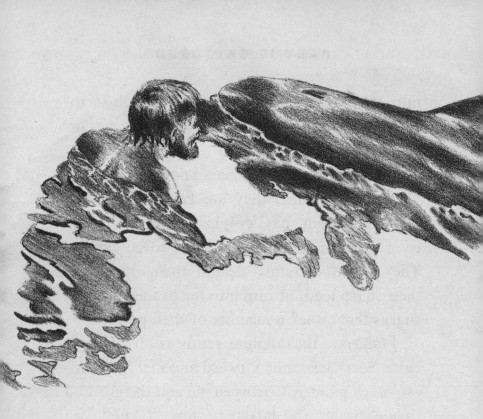

dying because a large fishhook was embedded in his body. As I had worked to remove the hook and save the baby, I had felt as if the dolphins were communicating with me.

At the time I didn't believe in such things, but I never forgot the way I kept sensing the dolphins were sending me messages. Something had happened that day that had made the dolphins adopt me as a friend.

Now they needed me again, and I was going to do my absolute best to help these intelligent creatures and find my missing friend Baby.

I treaded water very slowly, wondering what I could do to ease the dolphin's suffering. In my mind I saw the whole scene as the poachers ran down and netted Baby and the other missing dolphins. No wonder Papa and the others were sad and distrustful. I was a man, and men had taken away part of Papa's pod.

One of the poachers must have stuck a gaff hook deep into him as he tried to save his family. I felt tears welling in my eyes.

Once when I was lost at sea after a treasure dive, the dolphin family had saved me by taking me to shore during a terrible storm. I had had dreams as I passed in and out of consciousness, towed along on Baby's back. I had thought the dreams were hallucinations induced from fatigue and exhaustion, but now I remembered how vivid they had been.

In those dreams, I was a dolphin too, able to race through the water and dive deep. I had felt a sense of belonging and freedom I had never known before. I had the same depth of feeling now, but this time it was a feeling of dread and sadness. I knew something was terribly wrong.

I forced myself to keep thinking calm, loving thoughts, over and over, hoping to communicate peaceful understanding to the dolphins.

Scarback chirped loudly and bobbed his bottlenose up and down. Then the others chirped too. Scarback moved, and I could see Papa again.

I swam over to him and said, "It's okay now, Papa. I won't hurt you."

I stroked his broad head a few times, letting my hands run slowly down his back toward the high dorsal fin. His eyes followed my every move. He felt hot to the touch. Fever! I moved back a bit so I could see the hole in his side. It was small with a slight oozing of blood coming from it. I carefully felt the hole with my finger.

It was deep, deeper than my finger. Papa was so weak he could hardly stay afloat. His eyes, small and round, kept slowly closing. The old boy was in a bad way. I felt so helpless there in the sea alone with an injured creature I admired and respected. There was nothing I could do, but I knew dolphins are strong and have incredible recuperative powers.

For several minutes I stroked and talked to Papa. He lay quietly, moaning from time to time.

Bambi barked from above in the boat, and I knew I had to get back aboard before I drifted too far away. I said, "Good luck, Papa," swam to the trailing rope, and hauled myself back to the swim platform.

I looked out at the dolphins just in time to see two of them, Scarback and another male, take Papa between them and swim slowly away. I didn't know if he could survive, but I tried to convince myself he would make it.

Now I knew. Baby and the others were either penned aboard the catch boat or had already been delivered to the holding tanks on Dead Man Cay.

I decided right then and there that I would find Baby and the others and free them. But I would need help. A plan was already hatching in my mind by the time I pulled the *Treasure Hunter* into its slip at the marina.

Chapter Three

Dolphin Prison

DEAD MAN CAY, THE BAHAMAS

The large white boat backed slowly into the slip as its twin diesel engine exhausts rumbled and sputtered, sending wisps of oily smoke along the water's surface.

"Tie us off," ordered the captain, a heavyset man of around fifty. A younger man, wearing a black T-shirt that said HARLEY DAVIDSON FOR-EVER jumped across from the bow to the dock and quickly tied the boat to the cleats.

"Okay, Captain, she's moored tightly."

Hearing that, Captain Dirk Sanchez turned two keys and shut down the engines. "Get the forklift over here. These dolphins don't look too good. I want them put into the holding area right now before one of them croaks."

Trotting along toward a rusty old forklift parked near the dock, the deckhand answered, "Yes, boss. Don't want to lose these big fish like the ones last year, do we?"

Scowling back at his hired hand, Captain Sanchez said in disgust, "Animal, stupid. Dolphins are animals, not fish."

"Uh, yeah, boss, animals. Not fish."

Tommy Tyler was a good deckhand and a reliable helper, but after dropping out of school in the ninth grade, he knew little of the world except jobs of hard labor and trouble with the police.

Within minutes, Tommy had the forklift on

the dock, facing the rear of the *Big Blue*, a fifty-two-foot luxury yacht. The rear deck had been converted with shallow tanks for carrying live dolphins, suspended in the water on canvas slings with holes for their flippers to stick out.

The slings also kept the dolphins from trying to escape and held them mostly under the water so they could stay cool. Dolphins must breathe air like humans, so their blowholes on the tops of their heads were left exposed.

On the deck were five dolphins, lying quietly while running water kept their skin wet. Three other tanks were empty.

Baby and his mother, plus three more of his family pod, watched with anxiety as the men prepared to load their slings onto the forklift. Goofy, the one with the lopsided grin, was first. Tommy lowered the forks until they were even with the metal rack suspending the sling beneath it.

As soon as the fork was under the rack, it lifted the heavy male dolphin up in his sling until he was clear of the boat's side rail. Slowly the forklift backed off, turned, and made its way toward a concrete enclosure about fifty yards away.

"Okay, big fish, here's your new home." Tommy pushed the down lever, lowering the dolphin to the surface of the water in the tank. The other deckhands pushed it until it slipped out of the sling and into the water.

Instantly the dolphin dived, trying to escape—but he hit his nose on the rough concrete bottom, only twelve feet below.

Within a second, he was back on the surface,

blood streaming from his nose.

"Hey, Tommy, this dumb fish is bleeding bad," shouted Carlos, one of the men who had dumped Goofy from the sling.

"Better not let the boss know, Carlos; he'll be furious," said Tommy. "If that critter dies, he'll lose a lot of money. Get the rest of them over here pronto so they won't be so afraid."

Baby was the next to be unloaded. As his sling was lifted, he struggled violently to escape, almost causing the forklift to dump him onto the ground.

Carlos grabbed him by his dorsal fin and shoved him back into the sling. Baby let out a loud dolphin cry that sounded like a whistle. Carlos drew back his fist and hit him between the eyes, sending pain and fear through Baby.

"Now you know who's boss, big boy!" grunted the deckhand.

"Hey, man," shouted Tommy from his seat on the forklift. "You didn't have to do that. The poor fish is scared, that's all."

Glowering back, Carlos answered, "Mind

your own business. I know how to make these
dolphins behave. They need to know who is boss
right from the first."

Tommy took Baby to the pond and gently
lowered him to the surface while Carlos shoved
him out. The moment he was in the water, Baby
and Goofy started making noises that sounded
like whistles and grunts to the three men watching them, but to the dolphins, the sounds were
language to find out how each was.

As the last of the five dolphins was placed in the tank, the other dolphins stayed close and chattered among themselves. Baby's mother examined Goofy's hurt nose closely. Bluebell, Baby's youngest sister, nuzzled close to his side, making soft sounds of concern. She was the youngest and smallest of the five captive dolphins. Angel, the female born the year before Baby, was nearly as big as he was. The other male was from another pod of dolphins that traveled with Baby's family. He swam back and forth from edge to edge of the concrete enclosure, trying to find a way to freedom.

There was no way out. Strong wire mesh was strung over the holding area so the dolphins could not jump more than five feet without hitting it. There was no more freedom, no more roaming the open seas. They were captives of man, destined to be separated and shipped to amusement parks across Mexico and the Bahamas.

Captain Dirk Sanchez stood and looked at his latest catch and smiled broadly. "Twenty-five thousand dollars, maybe thirty," he said to himself. "Not a bad day's work."

JUPITER, FLORIDA

"I'm sorry, Mr. Grover, there's nothing we can do about the dolphin poachers once they have left United States waters. Even if we caught them here, getting evidence is nearly impossible. They just dump the dolphins when they see a patrol boat coming. Better to just forget it."

I turned and walked from the Florida Marine Patrol office, frustrated that there was no one willing or able to help stop the heartless dolphin thieves who roamed the offshore waters, hitting and running before being seen.

All that day, I worked on the *Treasure Hunter*, keeping busy while thinking over what to do.

About dusk, Amos drove up in his rusty old Ford pickup and stopped next to the dock. Grimacing with stiffness, he stepped onto the boat.

"I couldn't stop thinking about Baby and his family. It will never be the same without him to go along," he said as he settled into a deck chair next to me.

I looked from Amos's weathered face to the beautiful scarlet sunset lighting up the western sky. Two pelicans sat nearby, hoping for a handout of fish from the returning fishing boats docking near us.

"Amos, if the government can't help, then it's

up to us to find Baby and his family and free them. And we have to move fast, before they are sold and sent to marine parks. You know how horrible some of those parks are. Can you picture Baby or Bluebell doing flip-flops for dead fish?

"I'm determined to go after them," I said. "Do you want to go?"

Amos, tired after a hard day's work and feeling pain in every joint from his arthritis, thought about the question before answering.

"Wayne, it will be dangerous and require some pretty tight planning, but if you want this old man to help, count me in."

"Thanks, Amos. I called Jack today, and he's coming too. He loves those dolphins as much as we do. He just never says much about it. I figure we'll head for Dead Man Cay Friday night."

"If we find them there, you got any plans on how you're going to get them out?" asked Amos. "Those poachers are mean dudes who wouldn't hesitate to shoot us. We need a *really* good plan, because I don't want to catch lead poisoning."

"We have to get there first," I pointed out. "We'll look over the area and work out how to pull it off. Jack was in the Army Special Forces, and he knows a lot about covert activity. He'll do anything to help us get the dolphins back."

DEAD MAN CAY

The sun beat down on the concrete enclosure, raising the water temperature to around ninety degrees. Baby and the other dolphins lay under the shade of a wooden footbridge that spanned the gap between the pool and a narrow channel cut into the limestone, leading to the open Atlantic, about a hundred yards away. With the rise and fall of the tides, fresh seawater kept the dolphin pool filled.

Goofy's nose was red and raw. Baby and Mama, along with Bluebell and Angel, stayed in physical contact, resting motionless in the shade. Three times during the past twenty-four hours, Sanchez's men had thrown dead fish to them—

which they ignored completely.

The dolphins had never eaten dead fish and refused even to get near them. The rotting fish and the sun's heat combined to create a green scum on the water's surface, a sickly brew that could quickly endanger the dolphins' health.

"Pull that big male out here. I want to get a video of him to send to a customer." Sanchez pointed to the non-family male, which had made several cursory underwater explorations of the holding tank before settling down to hide with Baby and his family.

Carlos lowered a long pole with a loop suspended from the end and tried to slip it over the dolphin. Instantly the dolphin dived and shot across the pool until reaching the other end, fifty feet away.

It then swam around the perimeter as fast as it could go, barely missing the rough concrete walls as it did.

"Okay, mister!" shouted Carlos. "You asked for it."

Taking a big net in his hands, Carlos poised

himself above the pool edge and dropped the net over the dolphin as he swam by. Being trapped in a net for the second time in two days was too much for the male. He struggled violently and thrashed in the water. Carlos jumped in, grabbed the net, and started to tow it toward Sanchez. As Carlos was dragging the heavy load, Goofy shot out from under the platform and hit him hard in the side, knocking him away from the net.

Surprised and swearing, Carlos shouted to Sanchez, "Give me that stunner. I'll show this guy who's the boss here." The stunner is an electrical cattle prod, used on ranches to move reluctant cattle along chutes.

In the water, its shock was even worse when applied to a dolphin's back. Carlos had killed a dolphin the year before as he tried to force it onto a sling with the stunner.

"Don't get carried away, Carlos," warned Sanchez. "I want that dolphin alive."

The angry deckhand held the prod out of the water and took aim, hitting the netted dolphin right behind the blowhole. The shock stunned

the poor animal, sending waves of pain coursing through his body.

The dolphin lay still, too stunned to call out to the other dolphins nearby. Goofy lay close and watched before starting toward Carlos again. As he did, Carlos used the prod's heavy metal pole to smash down on Goofy's head, sending sharp pains up his bottlenose.

Goofy retreated to the shade with Baby and the females, where he lay quiet, still aching from the blow.

"Now that's more like it," said Carlos.

Sanchez turned on his video camera as the netted dolphin was freed and lay quietly on the surface, too scared to move.

The confrontation was over. The dolphins learned not to challenge the humans again.

Baby was confused. His relationship with his human friend, Wayne, had not prepared him for such a situation. He stayed back, and when it was his turn to be filmed, he meekly swam out with a little push from Carlos.

Five days later, with darkness falling, Amos steered our other boat, *Moon Shadow*, toward the Bahamas on a course of 155 degrees. Jack Riley sat and stared at the stars. I sat across from him, listening to the hum of the powerful engines driving the boat ahead at a steady forty-five miles per hour.

"We'll get the dolphins back. I've done a lot harder things in the army," said Jack.

I nodded my head, deep in thought.

I felt the same strange sensation I had had during my first contact with Baby's mother and father, the day I was called on to save their little dolphin's life. I had the feeling the dolphins could somehow reach me in some unknown way.

"Jack," I said softly, "I think Baby is telling me about their predicament. It's like the other times."

"I used to think you had read too many science-fiction novels, Wayne, but I stopped doubting after that day the dolphins saved you in the storm. Who knows what is possible? We shouldn't automatically doubt everything we don't understand.

"I've read books that say dolphins have saved many seamen over the years, and there are places in Polynesia where children and wild dolphins play together every day.

"If you say Baby is talking to you in some strange way right now, I say answer him back."

As I sat in the darkness, I tried to open my mind to receive anything that came from outside of my own imagination. I felt a sense of loss and sadness, as if I had lost one of my own family. The feeling was so strong it had to be real.

At midnight Amos asked me to take the wheel so he could go forward and get some sleep. We were already in sight of the Bahamas, and I turned south to track toward Dead Man Cay.

With Amos in the V-berth and Jack asleep on the open deck in a sleeping bag, I steered with the compass and watched the stars come and go as the tropical clouds blotted them out.

At around two-thirty, I heard a familiar sound, then another. It was dolphins chirping and blowing.

I flicked on the running lights and there in the sea, no more than twenty feet away, was the largest school of dolphins I had ever seen. They were moving toward Dead Man Cay as a group, swimming rapidly. I recognized Papa and Scarback, leading the large pod.

It became immediately clear that they were up to the same thing we were. They were headed directly toward Dead Man Cay, which told me that was where Baby must be held.

I decided to let the dolphins lead the way because their sonar and echolocation were even

better than my GPS.

I looked at the boat speedometer. The dolphins were swimming around forty miles per hour.

"Are we there?" Amos asked sleepily from the cabin.

"Not yet, but we've got company. Dozens of dolphins. Looks like several families have joined us."

Amos was quiet again. Then I heard his loud snore.

By five, we were off the coast of Dead Man Cay. I slowly cruised toward the lights on shore, wondering what I could do to free my friends.

Chapter Four

A Scary Island

"Amos, Jack, wake up. We're offshore from Dead Man Cay," I whispered to my two sleepy companions.

"Let's go into the main dock, there on the left," said Amos, pointing to a big SHELL OIL sign that flickered, illuminating the water near it. "As far as anyone is concerned, we're just three fishermen out for a Bahamian holiday."

The sun was just rising on the eastern rim of the Caribbean Sea, casting its crimson glow over the calm blue water of the Bahamas. As I looked eastward to admire the beautiful sunrise, I could see the dolphins that had come all the way from the Florida coast. Except for Papa, they lay quietly in the water.

Papa swam around the pod several times, acting agitated and nervous. Then he dived and was under for about two minutes. As he broke the surface, his breath exploded from his blowhole. I was relieved to see he was healing and seemed much better.

He clicked excitedly, and the others clicked back. He looked directly into my eyes as he came close to the boat and raised up on his tail, nodding his head while chirping loudly. I knew instantly what was going on. Papa had dived and sent his sonar echo directly toward the island.

Evidently his sound waves were heard and answered, because he was very excited. Within seconds the whole pod was nervously swimming in circles. I knew that meant the holding tanks were connected to the open sea by water, allowing the pod to communicate with their captured family members.

I too felt they were close. "The dolphins are here!" I said with authority.

Amos and Jack looked at me with that look of questioning they so often used when I told them about "communicating" with dolphins.

"Okay, Wayne, if the dolphins are here, I'll never doubt you again," said Amos. "These other critters are excited about something. We may have hit the target the first time."

Jack carefully scanned the shore with binoculars.

"I see a small inlet there to the south with a narrow channel cut right into the island. Looks like someone's using tidal flow to bring seawater inland. We'll look there first."

"I've heard about this island since I was a boy," said Amos. "It was used by English pirates during the sixteenth century. From what I hear, its current population is not much friendlier. We'll have to step with care so as not to arouse suspicion."

As we went toward shore, the dolphin pod left us and moved south about a half mile out.

"I'll bet they are doing the same thing we are," whispered Jack. "They're looking for a way to help their family."

Slowly Amos took the boat to a shabby-looking dock that was leaning to one side. Covered with barnacles, the exposed pilings were signaling low tide. As we pulled close to tie off, an old black man with white hair came out to look us over.

"Good-looking boat, mon. Where you from?" he asked with the typical Bahamian accent.

"Out of Jupiter, Florida," I said, smiling back. "Hope you've got plenty of gas. We're near empty."

"No problem, mon. We got plenty of gas," he replied. "Out fishing, are ya?" he added.

Amos squeezed my arm before I could answer and said, "Yup! Heard the groupers were running out here so we thought we'd party a bit and catch some big ones."

"Plenty of places to have a good time here," the man said. "My name is Julius. I'm the dock master. Let me know what you need and I'll point you to it."

The old Bahamian man helped us tie down. While he gassed the boat, I took a look around and noticed several Zodiac rafts scattered among the rotting fishing boats, and in the distance, at a private pier, I saw a large luxury yacht. It had to be the dolphin hunters' boat, I thought, but it was too far away to read the name.

As we walked down the dusty, rutted road leading to the village, we saw the old man pull out a small two-way radio and call someone.

"There's more to old Julius than meets the eye," said Jack, with a grim squint to his eyes. "You can bet whoever runs this island knows we are here by now."

It was nearly eight o'clock when we entered the village. We were only two hundred miles from Florida, but it seemed like another continent. With their paint faded and peeling badly, the old wooden buildings looked ready to fall apart.

The air was thick with charcoal smoke curling from little tin chimneys as breakfasts were cooked over coals. In the distance we heard the sound of dogs barking.

As we neared the little town center, several men came toward us, walking side by side, blocking the street.

"Uh-oh, looks like we drew a crowd already," said Amos under his breath. "They look pretty tough."

We kept walking, hoping they would go on past, but they didn't. When we reached a point right in front of them, we had to stop because they blocked the width of the street.

A tall man dressed in dirty jeans and a T-shirt full of holes looked me right in the eye and said, "What have we here? Three gentlemen from the states, over for a little fun, are you?" he asked, never taking his eyes off us. There were seven men in all, each watching us intently.

"Just out to catch some fish and take a weekend off," I replied.

The big guy looked at Amos and said, "Don't

I know you from someplace, old man?"

"Not that I know of," my friend answered.

"You really look familiar. . . ." He strained to remember where he had seen Amos but came up blank. "Where are you gentlemen going so early in the morning?" he asked.

I spoke up. "To get a good Bahamian breakfast. Where's a good place to eat?"

He seemed to relax and after a pause, said, "Just down there on the right, Captain Kidd's Tavern. The food is the best on the island. Tell them Gregor sent you."

"Thanks, I will," I said, forcing a phony smile.

Slowly the men parted and let us pass.

After they were out of hearing range, Amos said, "That was the inspection party. We haven't seen the last of them, you can bet. That guy Gregor was running one of those Zodiacs we saw off Jupiter. He remembers me because with my white beard I look like Santa Claus. They may have recognized you too, Wayne. It won't take any brains for them to figure out why we're here."

Settled in at Captain Kidd's, we had a breakfast of eggs and small fish, with fresh-baked rolls on the side. The table was dirty and the silverware spotted, but the food tasted great after a night at sea.

By nine-thirty, we were back at the boat. We bought some bait fish from the dock master and pulled away as if we were going fishing.

"There's no way we can snoop around this tiny place in daylight without arousing suspicion," I said as we cruised slowly across the glassy sea.

"Look over there." Jack pointed. "The dolphins are gathered offshore near that narrow canal that goes toward those buildings. I'll bet that goes right to the pens. It's the only way they could get enough seawater to keep the pools filled."

I raised the binoculars and looked at the dolphins in the distance. There were more than before. "Hey, the pod is growing. There must be fifty dolphins there off the coast," I said.

Amos squinted as he looked too. "Do you suppose Papa's pod has called for reinforcements?"

he said. "Looks like a gathering of the clan."

We cruised seaward, fishing lines trailing from outriggers, hoping we looked like regular fishmermen out for a weekend jaunt.

"I've got a plan," announced Jack. "We'll fish until late afternoon, then go back and tie up. We'll tell Julius we're sleeping aboard so we won't be watched so closely.

"After dark, we'll eat at Captain Kidd's and order up some rum and Coke. I want them to think we're plastered, but we'll pour the stuff out any way we can. If we sit near those potted palms by the street side, we can just dump it out into them. We've got to keep clear heads.

"Amos, you and Wayne start back to the boat while I stay and create a diversion. When the coast is clear, take a good look at the area where that canal comes inland, and remember what you see. Unless I miss my guess, the pool will be open to the sea except for some kind of net or bars for the water to pass through.

"If that's the case, all we have to do is cut through with the bolt cutters we've got on board, shoo out the dolphins, and run for it. Any questions?"

Amos and I looked at each other. "What kind of diversion?" I asked suspiciously, knowing Jack's reputation for having "fun."

"I'll think of something," he said with a smile.

"Deal," Amos and I said in unison.

At five-thirty, we started back to the dock with several fish we had managed to catch. The dolphins were nowhere in sight as we neared the island.

After tying up, we gave Julius his choice of the catch, a tradition in the Bahamas. Then we washed in fresh water from a hose and went to town for dinner.

Captain Kidd's was near full. It was a scene straight out of an old swashbuckler movie, complete with bearded, long-haired, tough-looking men and even tougher-looking women. Music was playing and drink was flowing.

All the men we had seen on the street earlier were there, plus more. Every eye was on us as we found a table on the outdoor deck near the street. Gregor, their grim-faced leader, stared at us as we sat down.

We ordered several rum and Cokes and made a big deal of pretending we were drinking them, acting drunk after the third one.

It grew dark as the noisy party of locals livened up. After we finished eating, we joined in some songs making the rounds of the place.

Each time we got a new drink, we casually poured it into the palm tree next to the table. The plan was working well so far.

By nine-thirty, the whole place was wild and noisy. Gregor was arm wrestling man after man, slamming their arms down on the tabletop.

"I think I'll try Gregor myself," I said with a wink. "He looks pretty soused."

Jack raised his eyebrows and said, "Who knows? You might beat him. Amos and I have never been a match for you."

"Hey, Gregor," I called across the room. "How about giving me a chance?"

The big man looked at me bleary-eyed and shouted, "Sure thing, city man. Think you can beat old Gregor?"

I went to his table, sat down, and was almost knocked back by his alcohol breath.

"Okay, mon, let's see what you've got," he grunted.

We put our elbows on the table, interlocked hands, placed our forearms together, and strained. What Gregor didn't know was that I had never lost an arm-wrestling match. I had worked at it since I was a kid growing up in Texas.

With a look of grim determination on his face, Gregor strained mightily and grunted. My arm did not move.

"Hey, boss, the city guy's arm is still up," said a scraggly companion nearby.

Gregor said, "Now you lose, my friend," and gave it his all.

My arm moved down and I felt my muscles straining to the breaking point, but I held it away from the tabletop.

For a full minute, we locked in battle. I took a deep breath and looked Gregor right in the eye. "Here's one for clean living." I pushed with all my might. I felt him give just a bit, and I pushed even harder.

With a loud grunt, he gave up and his arm slammed to the table. He looked at me and said, "A surprise from a city man. What other surprises do you have for me?"

By eleven o'clock, Gregor was still angry. "How about another match?" he challenged.

Jack stood up and said, "I guess you guys are pretty tough. Here's a bet. I don't arm wrestle, but I'll take on any three of you, right here, right now! One hundred dollars each says I can beat all of you."

"Aha, American, you make jokes," replied Gregor. "Arm wrestling is one thing, but fighting is a man's sport—and you look like a boy to me."

Jack was unperturbed. His clean-cut, youthful looks belied his years of martial-arts training in the Special Forces and later, as owner of a karate school.

"Which three?" asked Jack.

Gregor pointed to three burly men, who stepped forward as the others cleared the wooden floor and stood in a big circle.

Jack stepped into the circle and stood calmly.

"Show this kid how a real man fights," ordered Gregor.

Without warning, one of the three lunged at Jack, his fist cocked to strike out. He never saw what hit him. Jack sidestepped the rush, then pushed the man's arm up and away with his left hand while slamming his right elbow into his jaw. The man dropped, out cold.

The other two men rushed Jack as one. Like a ballet dancer, Jack spun around, bringing his foot into contact with one man's head while sticking his fist into the other's solar plexus, knocking all the wind from him. Both men dropped in a heap.

Barely breathing hard, Jack said, "Next."

Gregor looked stunned. "Perhaps I have underestimated you Americans. Come, let me buy you all a drink."

It was time to put the plan into action. I yawned and said, "I'm ready for bed."

Amos took the cue and said, "Me too. Your rum was too much for us. Come on, Jack, let's go back to the boat."

"You two go back. I've still got a few guys here who want to give me their money. I'll be back later."

Gregor smiled and said, "Mister Tough Guy, huh? Let's have a drink."

Amos and I staggered out, leaning on each other for support.

Gregor shouted after us, "Real men would stay and drink with us."

Once we were away from the restaurant, we looked around. The streets were empty. We stood up straight and smiled. "Okay, let's see what real men can do to find Baby and the others," I said.

Ahead in the darkness, we could see a foggy halo around several lights near the tin-roofed buildings we had seen earlier. Carefully we made our way until we were next to the largest building. There were no guards around.

Finding the door locked, I saw an open window and we crept over to it. I stood and looked inside. There, in a series of small concrete pools, each one connected by water but with a drop door to keep them apart, were at least twenty dolphins.

"Amos, look at this," I whispered.

He peered in. "There they are. And look how many."

"Keep watch, old friend, I'm going in."

I eased myself through the window, feeling the sweat running down my back. Once inside, I smelled a horrible stench. Dead fish were floating in each pool. The first dolphin I came upon just lay there in the water and stared blankly at me. The next several did the same. The poor creatures were too stunned and weak to do much more than breathe.

The large room under the tin roof was dimly lighted, but I could see dolphin fins in every holding area. The main pool ran outside, where I saw several other dolphins in a concrete pool with no roof over it.

I crawled along, looking into each area, whispering to each trapped dolphin. As I moved to the outdoor pool, I suddenly heard a loud chirping.

I looked down, and looking right back at me was Baby. His eyes danced, and he tried to swim to me. But he was held in place by the bars of the enclosure.

"Poor Baby, you look miserable." I reached down and stroked his head. He raised to meet my touch. "I'm going to free you, Baby. I promise."

I looked around and there, two enclosures away, were Mama, Angel, and Bluebell. The poachers had caught so many dolphins they had to double them up in the small cages with barely enough room to turn. I quickly counted twenty-four dolphins crammed into the enclosures off the main pool.

As I looked around, Baby kept making noise, excited to see me.

"Shhh, Baby," I softly called out. All the dol-

phins started chattering. I knew I had to get out fast before someone heard and came to investigate.

I went back out the window and told Amos what I had seen. "Come on, let's get back to the boat," I said quietly.

Within ten minutes we were back, carefully taking a side street to miss the saloon. By one-thirty, Jack was back too.

"How did it go?" he asked. We told him what we had found.

"We'll try to free them around three this morning. That way everyone should be sleeping," I said, whispering in case anyone was near the dock listening.

"If that guy Gregor remembers who I am, we're in for big trouble," Amos said with a sigh. "He's just small fry in this dolphin-poaching game, but he works for the big boss and he can cause us real problems."

Chapter Five

A Snag in the Escape Plan

It was three A.M., and the docks were deserted and the town was quiet. Our plan was simple. Jack and I were going to open each enclosure, letting the dolphins flee to freedom.

Amos was to back the boat out quietly and move to the area where the channel in the limestone had been cut. Jack and I would slip into the water, swim to the gate, open it, and follow the dolphins out, pushing any reluctant ones that might be confused and block the narrow channel.

Amos started the engines as we kept a close watch for anyone curious about us. If anyone approached, we would act as if we were going night fishing and cancel the action until the next night.

With the engines burbling their exhaust into the water, I winced at how loud they were. For a few minutes, we waited, but thankfully, no one came.

"Okay, let's do it," said Jack. I nodded, and we slipped over the boat's rail and onto the rickety old dock.

We kept to the shadows as we made our way to the holding pens. Once there, we entered through a window. Each pen had a rusty bar that went through a retaining loop to lock the enclosure and block the dolphin from moving into the next area or into the main pool. I struggled to pull the first one up, and finally it gave.

The female dolphin didn't move. I reached down and pushed her out the door. She went to the main pool and swam around it slowly. Within seconds another, freed by Jack, joined her.

One by one we opened the cages, and soon the main pool held nineteen dolphins. All that were left were Baby, Bluebell, Mama, Angel, and Goofy in the larger cage off toward the channel cut into the far end of the pool.

I slipped into the water, followed by Jack. We swam through the excited dolphins, gently pushing them aside to reach the last cage. "Are you sure all these critters are friendly?" whispered Jack.

As we reached the last cage, Baby was pressed against the bars waiting. He whistled and chirped excitedly, followed by the whole group sounding off.

"They're gonna wake the dead. Can't you do some dolphin talk and quiet them down?" asked Jack.

It sounded like a station full of whistling trains as each dolphin chattered.

"Too late now. Let's get this thing open," I replied as I tried to pull the last bar from its loop.

Jack grabbed it and tugged with all his might. It came free with a jerk and Baby rushed out, followed by the others. He put his nose in front of my face and nodded his head several times in quick succession.

His dolphin smile seemed broader than ever. Nose to nose, we looked into each other's eyes.

I patted his head and said, "Come on, Baby, we've got to move fast."

The main pool was cut into the limestone base that formed the small island, reinforced with concrete to keep the water from oozing out of the porous material. Twenty-four dolphins and two men swam toward the last obstruction to freedom, the big iron gates across the channel to the open sea.

Finally Jack and I reached the gate, surrounded by the dolphins. The channel was about eight feet wide and ten feet deep at low tide to allow the seawater to flow back into the pool. There was room for Jack and me and one or two excited dolphins near the gate.

We expected the main gate to the sea to have

a hinge we could cut, but a quick examination proved we had guessed wrong. There was no gate at all. Heavy bars were cemented solidly right into the limestone walls. And it would take a bulldozer to pull them loose.

"Uh-oh, we're in a heap of trouble now," I said.

Jack pulled against the bars with all his might, but there was no way he could move them. I swam alongside and tugged at each bar one by one, but they were at least two inches in diameter and solidly secured in the limestone.

Suddenly we heard shouting coming from town and saw lights come on. "This is serious stuff, Wayne. Those guys will blow us away when they find the dolphins out of their cages. Got any ideas?"

We were trapped in the rocky channel, with the dolphins so close we could hardly move. I knew I had placed Jack in grave danger, and probably Amos too.

I climbed up on the iron bars and tried to see where the channel met the sea. It was pitch dark and I could see nothing.

"If we swim fast, we might make the shore and get to the boat, but we have to go now," said Jack as he climbed over the bars and dropped into the water on the other side.

"I'm not going to leave the dolphins until I get them all to freedom," I said, not knowing how I was going to do it. "You get to the boat and have Amos come as close to shore as he can. I have an idea."

"Wayne, give it up. It's over. Come on, let's go," Jack urged.

"Jack, go now," I ordered. He hesitated and looked at me in the darkness. "Go," I demanded.

"I'll have the boat in as close as we can get it. If those guys start shooting, we've got to leave you behind," warned Jack.

"I know, buddy. Now go. Stay as long as you can, then leave me if I'm not there when the fireworks start."

With strong strokes, Jack swam along the narrow channel while I struggled to come up with a solution. There was only one way the dolphins could get out. Each one would have to jump the bars and head for the open sea.

I stood on the crossbar, looking back at my dolphin friends. Baby and his mother and Bluebell were closest to me. I had to convince them to jump the bars . . . but how?

I raised my arm and made a sweeping motion over the top of the bars time after time. "Jump! Jump!" I begged.

The dolphins chirped and whistled and bumped into one another in the crowded channel.

I heard voices close by, shouting. "Check the dolphin pens. Shoot anyone near them!"

I recognized the voice of the captain from the *Big Blue*. Other voices shouted, and I saw flashlight beams sweeping across the area between town and the holding pens. I knew I was in real trouble.

The voices and lights came closer as I desperately tried to get Baby to jump the steel barrier. Then it struck me. I had to communicate the way the dolphins understood.

I pictured myself racing toward the gate and

jumping high over it. Again and again, I visualized it.

"Captain Sanchez, the dolphins are gone!" I heard a voice very close shout.

"Jump, Baby. Jump!" I urged. The dolphins quieted down and spread out toward the rough sides of the channel.

I waved my arm over the bar once more and called to Baby to jump. He swam away from the gate as other dolphins opened up a clear channel for him.

A shot was fired in the distance. It was now or never. Baby swam rapidly forward, left the water in a high arc, and jumped over the bars, landing with a splash on the free side. He chirped loudly and moved excitedly around the narrow channel.

Mama was next to hurdle the bar, followed by Bluebell a moment later. Then a fourth and a fifth dolphin landed with a splash.

I pointed my arm toward the sea and said, "Go, Baby! Go! Go to freedom."

As I stood to one side of the crossbar, dolphin after dolphin jumped over, inches from my face. I laughed as the water splashed by each passing animal ran down my cheeks.

I heard more shots. I saw the lights of the main pool building come on, illuminating the channel nearly to where I was.

Baby led the procession of dolphins toward the open end of the channel. The last dolphin cleared the enclosure, and I jumped into the water and swam behind it. It was maybe a hundred yards to the sea, and I swam with all my might. A shot hit the limestone near me and ricocheted off with a whine.

Two men were running along the channel wall, firing into the darkness. The dolphins outdistanced me rapidly as I swam frantically. A searchlight beam swept the water behind me, and more shots whizzed close.

I knew I could never make it to the sea before the running men caught me. It was bedlam. Gunfire, lights, shouting, and panic. I swam with renewed effort, but I was tiring fast. The open sea and safety were still far away.

Chapter Six

A Dolphin Family Reunion

I was near exhaustion; my arms felt like lead as I threw them ahead and pulled back the water, swimming toward freedom with everything I had. I could hear men talking close by, and several lights swept the area behind me.

The voices came closer, and I knew I would never make it. Then a light found me. I stopped swimming and looked up to see a man who was no doubt Captain Sanchez smiling down at me.

"So, American, you have let my dolphins go. I will get them back, but now I have you. Antonio, throw him a rope and pull him out."

I knew Jack must be just about reaching the boat. If I delayed the captain with my capture, he and Amos could get away.

"Those were not your dolphins. They are wild and free animals, not to be used to entertain tourists. You had no right to bring them here," I called up, blinded by the flashlight beam in my face.

"You speak to me of rights!" he answered. "It is you who have come to my island and stolen my property. We do not have trials here with judges and lawyers. I am the law, and I say you must pay for your crime. You have cost me much money, and I intend to make you pay before I kill you."

I was in a tight spot with no way out. The best thing I could do was delay long enough in hopes Jack and Amos could get far enough away to out-run the captain's search boats.

"Okay, captain, you win. You've got me," I called out.

A rope was thrown to me by a dark, curly-haired man. I could see him and the captain and one other man in the lights coming from a vehicle that was parked somewhere above me. I wondered if I could possibly overpower them, then immediately knew that was a dumb idea.

Although I was strong and fast, I was not trained in the martial arts like Jack. I had to face whatever they had in store for me.

Just then the captain's walkie-talkie came on. I heard a voice saying, "The American's boat is gone. What should we do?"

"So, your friends have abandoned you? Too bad. I will take good care of you. Hold on to the rope, and Antonio will pull you out."

The captain keyed his radio and said, "Launch the Zodiacs and the gunboat and find the other Americans. If they resist, shoot them."

"Yes, Captain," the answer snapped back.

I held on to the rope as it was pulled up but let go as I began coming out of the water. "I'm too tired to hold on," I lied.

"Then tie the rope around your waist, and we will pull you out."

"No, I won't do it."

"You stupid man. Do you think you can defy me? Antonio, jump in and teach our friend a lesson in Bahamian manners."

With a splash, the burly seaman landed next to

me as the man above kept his light on us. The man in the water hit me with his fist, causing me to see stars for a moment.

Now I was really angry. My fist caught the guy on the side of his head, missing his jaw. It hurt my hand, but before I could swing again, he grabbed me by my hair and shoved my head underwater.

I could not raise my head high enough to breathe, and I struggled desperately.

After maybe thirty seconds, he let me breathe. "Now, American, tie the rope around your waist," he demanded, way too close to my face.

I treaded water and tied the rope around me.

"Antonio, throw up the end," the captain ordered.

Grabbing hold of the thick rope, Antonio tossed the end up, where it was caught by the other seaman.

He spread his legs and pulled mightily. As my two hundred pounds came out of the water, he struggled to drag me up the side of the rough rock wall. There was no way he could do it without help.

With a grunt of disgust, the captain grabbed hold of the rope, and they heaved in unison.

The rope dragged the rock edge, creating more resistance, but inch by inch I was going up. As my feet came out of the water, I reached to keep my face from being dragged on the rock wall. My hand found a crevice.

I held on, adding more resistance. Both the seaman and the captain leaned close to the edge so they could pull me up the wall. In an instant, I knew what to do. I grabbed on to the rope with both hands and pulled suddenly. The unexpected tug caused both men to lose their balance and tumble into the water, one of them on top of me.

As I fell, I dived under the water and swam close to the bottom, toward the sea.

Sputtering and cursing, the three men splashed around, trying to find where I had gone. I quickly untied the rope from my waist.

I came up about fifty feet away. Both flashlights had been dropped when the men pulled me, leaving the four of us in the dark channel. Still there was enough dim light from above for them to see me.

"Get him," the captain ordered.

Both seamen swam rapidly toward me as I swam away. They were fresh and soon overtook me, grabbing my legs and ripping my shirt as they fought to disable me.

Antonio pulled out a large knife and held it to my throat, saying, "One more move, and I'll cut your throat."

I believed him. I knew my life was over.

The captain swam toward us, muttering, "Let me kill him."

Try as I might, there was no way to evade dying right there and then. Alone on a small dirty island at the hands of a band of dolphin poachers.

Suddenly, Antonio was thrust through the water away from me.

A large dolphin had come up from below, stuck his nose between Antonio's legs, and catapulted him up against the rock wall.

Before Antonio hit the water again, the second seaman was lifted up and pushed through the water so fast he left a wake.

"Get away from me!" shouted the captain just

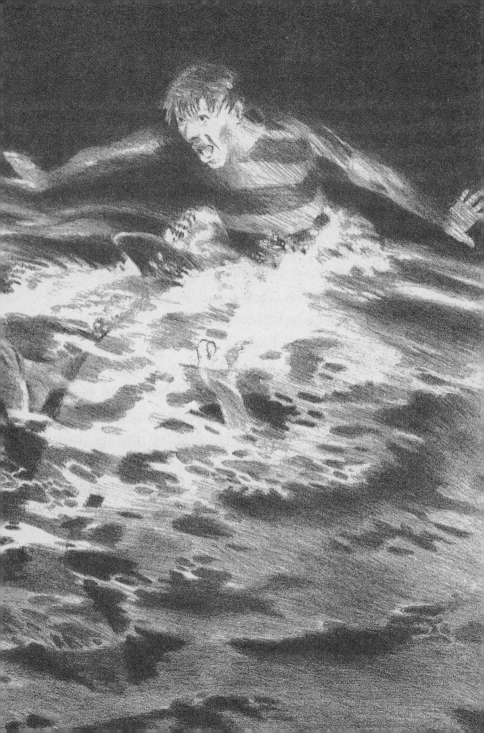

as he too was raised high on the nose of a third dolphin.

Several more dolphins surfaced and started pushing the three poachers back and forth between them. One swam to me, and I knew instantly it was Baby. He chirped excitedly and rose up to a tail walk amidst the splashing and shouting of the three human playthings being tossed around like dolls.

"Baby, you're incredible," I said, reaching out to stroke his broad head.

He nodded his head and blew a sharp exhalation from his blowhole. He fell back and rolled over with a splash. He pushed me with his nose, and I got the message. He wanted me to swim toward the sea and safety.

The captain and his thugs were trying desperately to get away, but the dolphins were enjoying the game too much to let them go. It was chaos in the channel as the dolphins each took a turn pushing the bad guys around and occasionally giving them a sharp boost into the air.

I knew the dolphins would not seriously hurt

the men, but they would be sore for a while. As I swam, Baby carefully put his nose against my rear end and pushed me along faster.

Within two minutes I saw the channel open out to a wider spot cut through the rock where the sea waves splashed across as they rolled to shore. Escape was at hand.

Baby pushed me right to the open sea so fast I kept getting water in my nose and mouth.

I could see the *Moon Shadow* rocking in the waves, but she was not alone. Three Zodiac rafts, each with a searchlight piercing the darkness, were racing toward her from the marina.

"Amos! Here!" I shouted.

Amos called out, "It's about time, old friend. We've got bad company coming fast!"

Baby shoved me right to the boat where Jack reached down, grabbed my arm, and jerked me on board.

The Zodiac rafts were nearly on us before Amos shoved the throttles to full speed ahead.

"Halt or we'll shoot!" came an order over a loudspeaker.

Amos hesitated a moment, and a shot hit the cabin window just to his right. He pulled the throttles to idle and the bow settled back down to the water.

"Don't move! Raise your hands over your head," the loudspeaker ordered.

We did. Jack and I looked at each other as Amos said, "Any ideas, guys?"

Each raft had two men and from the distance, we saw a Bahamian gunboat coming with a large searchlight sweeping the water ahead.

We were surrounded by gun-toting pirates and poachers intent on delivering us back to Captain Sanchez.

The Zodiacs bumped alongside our boat as two men with guns stood and prepared to come aboard.

Amos went into action. Even though he was well into his sixties, at six-feet-four and two hundred and fifty pounds, he feared nothing. Jack and I watched as he moved quickly to meet the first man who climbed aboard.

"Okay, matey, this is my boat, and you're not

invited to the party," he said as he grabbed and lifted the big man over his head and threw him overboard, his gun flying from his hand.

Splash! The guy hit the water.

The next man, holding on to our boat rail to keep the Zodiac with us, let go and grabbed a rifle from the raft's floor. He was a split second too late as Jack picked up our rope pole and shoved him overboard.

The second Zodiac, being held against the other side of our boat, suddenly lurched violently, knocking the two standing men into the water. Dorsal fins were everywhere as the dolphins joined the action, remembering the Zodiacs and the men who had captured them days earlier.

It was an amazing sight as the dolphins repeatedly hit the big rafts each time a man tried to climb back aboard. The third raft idling nearby met the same fate as five dolphins took turns banging it from the sides, sending its occupants into the water.

Just as they had in the channel, the dolphins pushed the men around with their noses in a game

of seamen soccer. I saw Papa lift one of them and send him tumbling head over heels. The old boy was paying them back for hurting his family, and he took great joy in scaring each of the men as they floundered in the dark water.

"Let's get moving! We can outrun that gunboat," shouted Amos as he shoved the throttles to full. The *Moon Shadow* leapt forward, causing Jack and me to grab on to the boat to keep from falling.

The big gunboat's searchlight came across the dark water and caught us in its beam. Amos immediately swerved the boat to the left, then the right, to get out of the light, but they had us spotted.

Boom! Splash! The gunboat fired at us, sending up a splash about a hundred feet behind. *Boom! Splash!*

"They're getting closer!"

Amos twisted and turned the *Moon Shadow* to throw off the gunner's aim.

Boom! Way off. *Boom!* So close it threw water onto the deck.

"Come on, horses," called Amos as he held the

throttles full forward, as if he could will more speed from the three two-hundred-and-fifty-horsepower engines pushing us.

We began to pull away.

Boom! The shot missed.

Boom! We heard the shell whistle close over our heads.

Boom! The shell landed farther away.

Boom! Way off. This time we knew we were pulling out of range. And fortunately none of the shells fell near the dolphin pod.

"Those guys are history," said Amos. "I'm sure glad I spent big bucks for these engines. Look at the speedometer. We're hitting seventy-two miles an hour. Not bad for an old pleasure boat."

"Amos, any boat with three two-hundred-and-fifty-horsepower engines is a long way from a rocking-chair pleasure boat," chimed in Jack. "I don't know a boat on the Florida coast that can outrun this tug, except some of those million-dollar, Miami, cigarette racing boats."

"Beat some of them too," Amos said with a laugh.

Within fifteen minutes, the gunboat was so far back we could barely make out its running lights. We were safe.

I took the wheel so Amos could sit down and get some much-needed rest. I steered straight for Palm Beach, Florida.

As we passed out of Bahamian waters into international territory, I relaxed and slowed down to a steady forty-five miles per hour.

"Wayne, I saw what happened back there with the dolphins, but I still don't believe it." Jack's mind was wrestling with a mystery each of us was thinking about.

"You know, don't you, that no one will ever believe this," I answered. "But it happened. You saw it. Baby came to our rescue and brought all his buddies."

Jack took the helm as the sun rose in a great red ball over an almost calm sea. On the horizon, I could see the skyline of Fort Lauderdale. We would be home in an hour. I lay on the deck in the cool morning air, yawned, and was asleep.

I awoke with the sun warming my skin. It felt

delicious after being wet and cold all night. We docked by ten A.M.

"Should we tell anyone about this?" Jack asked. "Maybe you should write a book about dolphins. This would make a heck of a story, but no one would believe it."

We called the Marine Patrol and told them we had freed twenty-four dolphins from Dead Man Cay.

"How did you manage that?" the lieutenant asked.

"With a little help from our friends," I said.

"I hope you didn't break any laws out there."

"Maybe we bent a few, but that's another story," I said, hoping he would not ask any more questions.

The officer added, "I bet we don't get any complaints from Dead Man Cay."

That evening, as I cleaned up the *Moon Shadow*, I looked out and saw several dolphins arching through the water, coming toward our intracoastal mooring.

The dolphins usually don't enter the inland

waterway, preferring to stay in the open sea. But there they were. I felt like they were making a house call to say thank you.

I called out, "Babeeee!"

The pod swam toward me. Bambi and Blossom stood on the bow deck wagging their tails. They were happy to see our friends and saviors again too.

Baby, Mama, Papa, Bluebell, Angel, and Scarback came right to the dock while Goofy and three others stayed about a hundred feet away, watching.

I took off my shirt and shoes and jumped into the water to greet them. Baby came to me and chirped loudly, nodding his bottlenose up and down rapidly. He wanted to play. They all wanted to play.

I thought, What a lesson people could learn from these wonderful animals. They lead simple lives devoted to their family structure. They care for one another and protect their young and old from predators. They don't pollute, don't fight or hurt others unless their lives are in danger.

They had trusted people, but they nearly paid dearly for it. I felt guilty for having caused them so much trouble. In the dolphin world, they live in the present, react to the moment, and enjoy a life of absolute freedom.

Bambi jumped overboard and swam to me while Blossom watched and wagged. True to form, Baby picked Bambi up on his back, and she struggled to keep her footing. They toured the marina, bringing smiles to everyone who saw them.

Finally Bambi had enough and jumped off and

swam to me. Baby rose high in the water and tail-walked back and forth in front of us. Bluebell and Angel did the same. Mama and Papa were content to let the youngsters play with us land animals.

As the sun set in a blazing inferno of reds and golds, I sighed deeply, thankful to be a part of such a wonderful moment. A chance encounter with an injured baby dolphin eight years before had opened a doorway to a whole new understanding of what life should be.

"Thank you, Baby," I said. "Thank you."

WAYNE GROVER was born in Minnesota and has lived and worked on four continents. Endowed with a deep respect and fascination for nature and its conservation, he is most at home on a mountain or under the sea. Since 1966 he has dived for Spanish treasure in sunken ships off Florida and says he enjoys the historical aspects of the ventures more than any silver or gold he might find.

Mr. Grover is a national news correspondent and often lectures at schools on the need for conserving our natural resources and wildlife. His articles have appeared in newspapers and magazines around the world. He is the author of *Dolphin Treasure*, *Dolphin Adventure*, and *Ali and the Golden Eagle*. He lives in South Florida with his wife, Barbara, and their two dogs.

JIM FOWLER grew up in Tulsa, Oklahoma, and moved to Alaska in 1973. He enjoys kayaking, camping, and wildlife viewing. He is the illustrator of *Albertina the Practically Perfect, Beautiful, I'll See You When the Moon Is Full, When Joel Comes Home*, and *Fog*, all by his wife, Susi Gregg Fowler, and of *Dolphin Treasure* and *Dolphin Adventure* by Wayne Grover.

The Fowlers live in Juneau, Alaska, with their daughters, Angela and Micaela.